ESCAPADE JOHNSON
and
Phantom
OF THE
SCIENCE FAIR

written by
Michael Sullivan

illustrated by
Joy Kolitsky

PublishingWorks, Inc.
Exeter, NH
2009

PublishingWorks, Inc.

151 Epping Road

Exeter, NH 03833

603-778-9883

For Sales and Orders:

1-800-738-6603 or 603-772-7200

www.publishingworks.com

Designed by Anna Pearlman

LCCN: 2009920800

ISBN: 1-933002-52-2

ISBN-13: 978-1-933002-52-1

CURR
P2
7
.S95333
Esp
2009

Printed on recycled paper.

Printed in the United States.

INTRODUCTION

It's me again, Escapade Johnson, here in the most boring town in the entire state of New Hampshire. Winter was incredibly dull around here for a fifth grade boy who wants to be a writer. How can I become a famous author if I don't have anything to write about? I mean, you can only go ice fishing for so long before your boots freeze to the ice, and once you've sledded off old man Spoerl's roof a dozen times, it starts to lose its thrill. The most exciting thing that happened all winter was when I accidentally switched the heat off and turned the air conditioning on during a town meeting in January. By the time anyone noticed, all the doors and windows were frozen shut. They had to burn all the town tax records to stay warm until they were rescued the next day. Oddly enough, my parents didn't ground me or yell at me or anything. But that's another story.

Winter is over and with spring comes the annual fifth grade science fair at Sanbornton Elementary School. Sounds boring, I know, but this is Sanbornton, and the science fair is likely to be the most thrilling event of the season. Last year, Shayna Rhavin tried to breed a frog with two heads. She succeeded, but the heads were on opposite sides of its body so it didn't have anywhere to poop. By the time of the science fair, the frog was four weeks old and it hadn't ever gone to the bathroom, so it sort of exploded all over the judges. I tell you, that is a lot more exciting than ice fishing.

So here is my story, folks, complete with carnivorous gerbils, swimming books, lipstick-wearing rabbits, and the Phantom of the Science Fair.

Enjoy.

CHAPTER 1

"**A** thousand bucks!" Jimmy Whitehorse was wide-eyed, shaking his head and, I swear it, drooling from his wide-open mouth. "Man, I could, like, build the world's hugest skateboard ramp."

"No you couldn't," corrected Mr. Hauteman. "The prize is an educational savings bond. You could only spend it on college tuition."

"Still," said Jimmy, ever the optimist, "I bet I could sell it to someone who wanted to go to college for, like, eight hundred bucks. The ramp would still be massive."

"In what universe could you win first place in the science fair?" cried out Cherilyn. "You haven't done science homework all year, and you're using your science book to plug a hole in your doghouse. You said so just yesterday."

"I could win the science fair!" Jimmy sounded more angry than confident. "Anything's possible, I guess."

"Not this time," grumbled Davy. "Only one person has a chance in the science fair."

Everybody in the class turned to look at Melinda, including Mr. Hauteman, the science teacher.

"What?" Melinda cried, looking like a cornered animal.

Melinda was the best science student in the class. She was the best student period, but science was her extra-special favorite subject. To be fair, Mr. Hauteman was her favorite teacher. Whether Melinda loved him because she loved science, or she loved science because he taught it, no one could say, but it didn't matter. Melinda had been the only kid in Sanbornton looking forward to the fifth grade science fair all the way back in the third grade.

"Here's a test," Cherilyn continued. "What is your science experiment going to be?"

"The effect of classical music on various food plants," Melinda answered, as if by reflex.

"Wow," said Davy. "You figured that out in two minutes?"

"No, you dope," Cherilyn snapped. "She's been planning this for years. I bet she has diagrams of it in her notebook."

Melinda tried to slip her notebook into her backpack without anyone noticing.

"Who cares about what music plants like?" asked Benny Black.

"Depends on what type of plant you are trying to grow," chimed in Jimmy. "I remember my dad's friend Chuck spending weeks trying to figure out what lights would make the plants in his basement grow faster."

"Thank you, Jimmy," Mr. Hauteman said quickly. He was getting pretty good at knowing when to keep Jimmy quiet. "Melinda, why don't you tell us what types of plants you will be experimenting on?"

"Oh, lots of them: tomatoes, beans, garlic. I even have a miniature alfalfa plant." Melinda was warming to her subject. "I want to prove you can grow food faster if you play classical music, like symphonies and sonatas, near the plants. This could solve the problem of world hunger and the problem of people listening to bad music at the same time!"

Mr. Hauteman beamed at her enthusiasm, then seemed to remember that he isn't supposed to play favorites.

"Does anyone else have their science fair project picked out?"

Marjorie Jackson's hand shot up, knocking a pile of books and papers all over the classroom floor, which wasn't surprising. Marjorie is a bit of a klutz. Okay, a club-footed rhinoceros is a bit of a klutz; Marjorie is a walking disaster area.

"Yes, Marjorie. What do you have planned?"

"I want to find a way to control the reaction of potassium to oxygen."

The half of the class that didn't get chemistry looked impressed. The half of the class that did get chemistry just looked worried. Mr. Hauteman looked genuinely frightened.

"By 'control the reaction,' you mean 'control the explosion'?" Mr. Hauteman asked hesitantly.

Marjorie nodded.

"Coooollllll," breathed Jimmy, who had no idea what "control the reaction" meant, but knew what an explosion looked like. I had seen a few explosions that Jimmy had cooked up. I could only imagine what Marjorie's klutziness could do to make one of them worse.

"Do you think that is really such a great idea?" Mr. Hauteman continued. "I mean, that stuff has to be handled pretty carefully . . ."

The whole class spent a few heartbeats remembering Marjorie's history of drops, fumbles, trips, and goofs. She had grown too fast for her limbs to keep up, and nothing within their reach was safe. Marjorie managed to send a juggler sprawling from his unicycle at last summer's Old Home Day, spill Jell-O mold over all three selectmen at a school fundraising dinner, and break a record seventeen jigsaw blades in one class period of wood shop.

"What?" she cried, in response to the unspoken accusation. "I can do this, I'll be careful." The last statement was more of a plea. She looked pitifully at Mr. Hauteman, who seemed to struggle with the idea for a few seconds then sighed heavily.

"All right, it's your project. Just please be very careful. Very, *very* careful."

It was the first in a long line of ominous signs about a science fair that no one in Sanbornton Elementary School would soon forget.

CHAPTER 2

The next day, Melinda and Marjorie had their experiments in the lab and set up. Melinda had six sets of plants in pots, each separated by sound-deadening tiles and with its own radio set to a different classical music station.

"One station plays music from the Classical period, one from the Baroque period, one plays all Russian music, one all Hungarian, and there is a special station for Beethoven and another for Mozart."

Davy Gilman groaned. "Why not have some of the plants listen to heavy metal? I bet The Ax-Wielding Zombies could scare the plants into growing faster."

The whole class laughed, but Mr. Hauteman looked serious as he spoke to Melinda.

"Davy does have a point," he said. Melinda looked surprised. Davy himself looked shocked. I don't think he'd ever had a point in his life. "You should really have some kind of control group with which to compare your results," Mr. Hauteman continued.

"And subject them to that?" Melinda pointed to the gory scene silk-screened onto Davy's black

T-shirt that showed a long-haired, half-starved, guitar-wielding rock star pummeling a Volvo into submission. "That would be cruelty to plants."

Mr. Hauteman shrugged and moved on to Marjorie's table, though he made sure to stay safely back and peer from a distance. Marjorie had set up a beaker, stoppered and upside down, filled with a thick yellowish substance, and suspended in it was a small metallic glob. As we all watched and held our breath, Marjorie ran a tube from a small canister through the stopper. She turned a knob on the canister, and slowly a bubble of gas formed at the end of the tube inside the yellow sludge.

The bubble detached itself from the tube and floated slowly up until it collided with the metallic substance. There was a brief flash and the glob glowed bright yellow for a second or two. Not only were none of the windows of the school blown out, but the beaker itself was intact. Another bubble of oxygen started to form at the end of the tube. Mr. Hauteman released his breath.

"Marjorie, you may have something. Just make sure the covers stay on the potassium and the oxygen."

Marjorie looked prouder than I have ever seen her.

"Who else has a project to show us? Davy?"

Davy walked over to a large square-ish object covered in a cloth. He stood behind the table and whipped the cover off to reveal a large wire cage separated into two compartments. In each half of the cage, four fluffy little balls rolled and scrambled over each other in an explosion of energy.

"I, too, have a project about food," Davy began.

"Big surprise," whispered Benny, just loud enough for people in the next classroom to hear. But I was looking at Davy—a mountain in white basketball sneakers—and the gerbils, and wondering what food had to do with it all. The thought made me queasy. But Davy quickly put my mind at ease . . . then sent it reeling again.

"I want to see if people having to feed gerbils vegetables is all just a bunch of bull . . . scat." He looked pointedly at Melinda. "And I do have a control group." Again he looked at Melinda, who turned away in disgust. "This group will get fed a regular diet of lettuce and carrots and whatever other junk the cafeteria bothers to give me, while this group here will get fed hot dogs, pork ribs, and prime rib. We'll see which ones grow up big and strong."

Everyone in the class looked about nervously. Nobody ever wanted to run the risk of getting Davy mad, even most of the teachers, but this was such obvious madness it was hard to keep quiet. Mr. Hauteman eventually broke the silence.

"You do know, Davy, that gerbils are herbivores?"

"Well, yeah, but that doesn't mean they don't eat meat."

"Actually . . ." Katrina Finink started to object, but one worried look from Cherilyn cut her off.

Mr. Hauteman just sort of nodded, looking confused, and went on to the next table. There was Cherilyn with a cage of her own, a big one. In it were four rabbits.

"I have decided that some cosmetic companies are ruining it for all by cruelly testing their makeup on animals. I have a solution."

She paused dramatically. Mr. Hauteman waited for her to continue. She looked a little annoyed. I'm sure she expected him to ask fascinated questions, but she braced herself and plowed on.

"I think we should test makeup on animals in non-cruel ways!"

"So you aren't going to spray hairspray in their eyes?" asked Melinda.

Cherilyn shook her head and gave a big smile.

"You aren't going to put toxic chemicals on their shaved skin?" I asked.

Cherilyn shook her head and looked smug.

"Is that rabbit wearing lipstick?!" Benny asked, suddenly leaning out of his chair and peering into the cage.

"That's right!" beamed Cherilyn. "Bubblegum pink. I think it goes with its eyes. That one there is a male, so he's wearing my dad's cologne."

One second of silence. Two. Then the whole class erupted in laughter. Cherilyn glared around, but there were too many kids laughing for her to focus her razor-sharp stare on anyone.

CHAPTER 3

"Could the station have changed formats?" Mr. Hauteman asked, trying just a bit too hard to be helpful. Melinda looked crushed.

"Dunno, maybe." Her bottom lip was quivering and she was obviously trying not to cry. The little tomato plant in front of her was stunted, its leaves thick and yellow.

When the class had arrived in the science room, the first plant on her table was sitting beside a radio blaring "Guillotines Solved All My Problems" by a heavy metal band called The Skull Crushers.

Suddenly her eyes flashed and she wheeled, pointing directly at Davy with a finger that looked like it might be loaded.

"Of course, maybe he changed the channel. He wanted to torture innocent plants with that heavy metal garbage!"

If Davy had made an obvious effort to look innocent, I might have believed he was guilty. But Davy just looked really confused.

"I didn't touch it," he said. "I didn't even know that station existed, but it sure rocks!"

Melinda took two steps forward, her finger ready to poke a hole in Davy's chest, before Mr. Hauteman caught her by the arm.

"I don't think Davy changed the channel," said Mr. Hauteman. "When could he have? You must have just brushed the dial when you were setting it up yesterday. How bad is the damage?"

"One night of heavy metal music and that tomato plant actually grew bark, and it's so thick the plant will never grow right. It's stunted and warped. Can you imagine what that stuff will do to your brain if you listen to it day after day, year after year?"

She stared at Davy and said, "I can."

Mr. Hauteman changed the subject before Davy could work out exactly what that meant.

"Escapade, what have you got for us?"

I looked down at the preliminary plans I had made and swallowed hard. I had thought about teaching a computer to play chess, but I don't know how to play chess. I had looked at an experiment to make a liquid that changed colors at different temperatures, but my mom won't let me use dyes ever since I turned my sister Revelation's hair purple. In the end, I had gone with the only project that was left.

"Um, I was going to make a working volcano."

Snickers came from around the room.

Mr. Hauteman frowned. "Let me guess, baking soda and vinegar?" I nodded. "Papier-mâché cone?"

Gulp. Nod. More snickers. I heard Benny whisper, "I did that one in third grade."

Cherilyn giggled. "Escapade did it in third grade too."

Mr. Hauteman stared down at me. "Escapade, that's a good enough project, but it has been done more than once. Have you considered doing something else?"

"I couldn't think of anything else."

And there it was. In what would become the most memorable science fair in all of history, I, the most boring kid in the most boring town in the most boring state in the whole country, had picked the most boring science fair project ever.

CHAPTER 4

Smoke seeped from the burnt edges of a ragged hole in the lab table where Marjorie's project had been the day before. It also poured from the burnt edges of a ragged hole in the floor beneath the lab table where Marjorie's project had been the day before. The whole class was gathered around the hole, and Jimmy would have fallen in if Davy hadn't stomped on his foot.

"You left the cover off your experiment," Mr. Hauteman said flatly, looking at the devastation in his science room.

"I didn't, I swear!"

"I have some evidence that you did."

Marjorie looked more miserable than she had the time she dropped beef stew all over Cherilyn on the very day that Cherilyn announced she was becoming a vegetarian.

"What evidence? Maybe it was something else. Maybe it was lightning!"

"From a cloud inside the school?" asked Benny, staring at the undamaged ceiling above.

"They found the bottle in the library, and the cover a few feet away."

"It burned all the way into the basement?" cried Jimmy Whitehorse, looking at Marjorie with real admiration.

"Yes," sighed Mr. Hauteman. "Right through a water pipe and into the library."

"A water pipe?" Marjorie squeaked.

Mr. Hauteman nodded. "A big one. Eighteen inches, a main line. Poured a couple thousand gallons into the library. *Moby Dick* floated right out the door."

A respectful hush fell over all the assembled fifth graders.

"What idiot put the library in the basement under a major water pipe?" asked Benny.

What idiot put *Moby Dick* in an elementary school library? I wondered.

Mr. Hauteman ignored Jimmy. "Marjorie, you have to learn to be less . . . well . . . more careful."

"I was careful! I checked that cap three times before I left yesterday. I swear I did."

Her voice trailed off to a whimper. Tears began to spring to her eyes. She covered her face and whipped around to face the wall, elbowing the roll-down Periodic Table of Elements in the process. The chart retracted with a loud bang, making everyone jump, then gasp at what was revealed.

On the concrete wall behind where the chart had been, painted in large red letters, were the words, "Chemistry is not for the clumsy. The Angel of Science."

"You see?" Marjorie leapt forward, throwing her hand out to point at the wall and sending a hanging skeleton flying through the air and landing in a full tackle on Jimmy. It took a few minutes, but Jimmy got the best of the skeleton by biting one of its legs. "I didn't mess up this time. Someone sabotaged my project."

There were murmuring cries of agreement, and a few of disbelief. Mr. Hauteman raised his hands for calm. "Wait a minute here. You were the last person out of the lab yesterday. I locked up just as you left. And I've been in this room since I opened up this morning. I don't know when that message was left, but nobody has been in this room since you left your experiment."

"Someone must have snuck in last night when everyone went home."

Mr. Hauteman shook his head. "We lock the science room at night. There are too many dangerous chemicals . . ." He paused and looked pointedly at the steaming hole in the center of the science lab. ". . . For us to take chances. There are only two keys. I have one, and Principal Lissard has the other. The custodians don't even get in here at night."

Marjorie still didn't look convinced. "There's something strange going on here."

"Yeah!" Benny jumped in. "For the last three weeks, my gym socks have been disappearing out of my locker!"

Everyone stared at him. I couldn't imagine what connection there could be between Benny's sweaty gym socks and dangerous chemicals . . . oh wait. I guess I could. Still, who would touch them?

"I mean this message. Something's up," said Marjorie. But the fight had gone out of her. She knew her reputation as the school klutz had just become a legend that would outlive us all.

Mr. Hauteman made us all find tables as far away from the hole as possible, and started asking other students about their projects.

"Katrina, we haven't heard from you yet. What are you doing for the science fair?"

It was then that I noticed something funny about Katrina. She looked oddly tired, or sleepy, or just out of it somehow. It was hard to say. Her eyes were red and didn't appear to be able to focus on anything.

"The science fair? Oh, something on energy, I think."

"That sounds interesting. Anything more specific?"

"Apples."

"Come again?"

"Apples."

"Apples and energy?"

"Yeah, I guess . . ."

Katrina hadn't guessed about anything in her life. Every statement she made was a definite, even if she had no idea what she was talking about. Something was definitely up.

Mr. Hauteman seemed to consider how to proceed. "And what inspired you to do your project on apples and energy?"

"It came to me in a dream . . ." Nervous glances all around. "I kind of fell asleep during study hall and when I woke up, well, there it was."

"Okayyyyyyyy. Um, Jimmy, what are you doing?"

"It's a secret," Jimmy said matter-of-factly.

"You aren't going to tell us yet?"

"I'm not telling anyone until the day of the science fair."

"Won't we know what you are doing when you set up your experiment?"

"I'm doing it at home."

"Really, so you are going to do your experiment at home by yourself and just bring it in on the day of the science fair?"

"That's right."

"And we are just going to trust that you are making good progress?"

"Absolutely."

"And we should just hope that nothing disastrous happens, like, say, your dogs eating your experiment?"

"Something like that," replied Jimmy with a mischievous smirk.

"Right. Okay, it's your grade. Davy, how's your project going? Any noticeable weight gain in your gerbils?"

Davy was already putting squirming gerbils into a box on a postal scale and making marks in his lab book. After a second he looked up, disappointment on his face.

"Yes, a little, but the ones eating vegetables are gaining just as much weight as the ones eating meat."

Mr. Hauteman peeked over the cages. "It's early yet. There's time for the results to fall out. How much of their food have they eaten?"

Davy leaned in too and grunted. "Doesn't look like they are eating much of anything."

"Really?" Mr. Hauteman looked surprised. "The vegetable group or the meat group?"

"Both."

CHAPTER 5

Benny leaned over the wooden maze he had built, a stopwatch in his hand. He had come into the room without a word to anyone and set up on a corner table. Everyone had watched him, but his back was turned to the rest of the class, and we couldn't see what he was doing. Finally, curiosity got the better of Cherilyn, or her basic busybody-ness, and she stepped up behind Benny.

"So what's your experiment?" she asked, trying to peer around him.

"It's military."

"Military?" asked Mr. Hauteman, sounding almost as concerned as he had been over Marjorie's experiment.

"Yes, I'm developing a new delivery system for nuclear weapons."

Hearing the words "nuclear weapons" come out of Benny's mouth had to be one of the most frightening experiences I have ever had at Sanbornton Elementary School, and I had once seen our gym teacher, Mr. Dobson, lose his shorts at the top of a rope he was showing us how to climb.

"Um," stuttered Mr. Hauteman, "you don't actually have any kind of live weapon, do you?"

"Of course not," Benny answered. I don't know if he sounded insulted or defensive. With Benny, it's hard to tell, mainly because it is easy enough to believe he would show up at school with some homemade version of a cruise missile. His years in New York City made him just a bit more comfortable with the idea of weapons, crime, gangs, and every other interesting subject than those of us who had grown up in small-town New Hampshire.

"I've made mock-ups of the bombs," Benny continued, "to scale, of course, and I am testing the delivery system using the duds."

"The delivery system?" Mr. Hauteman asked, creeping up to look over Benny's shoulder. Cherilyn had crept up, too, and when Benny turned to look at Mr. Hauteman she got a clear view of the maze and what was inside.

"Roaches!" Cherilyn screamed, and jumped up on a table, which was silly since the roaches weren't on the floor, they were on the same table she jumped on. Just reflexes, I guess, but girls just don't make a lot of sense to me.

"Of course, roaches," Benny continued calmly. "We've all heard that nuclear radiation won't kill roaches, so what better way to transport nuclear bombs than on roach-back? All I have to do is teach them to follow a determined route and drop their payloads."

"But, Benny," Melinda put in, sounding horrified. "Radiation won't kill roaches, but it does make them mutate. Have you considered the possibility that they will get, well, bigger?"

"Yeah," said Benny, with a huge smile on his face. "That's the best part. The more bombs they deliver, the more radiation they will be exposed to, the bigger they will get, and then they will be able to carry bigger and bigger bombs."

Mr. Hauteman's mouth moved, but nothing came out. He was still mouthing inaudible words and rolling his eyes as he turned his back on Benny's table and found himself facing Katrina's. It was one week before the science fair, and Katrina's experiment already looked like something from a science fiction movie. There were tubes, beakers, spigots, Bunsen burners, and copper piping. Apple peels were simmering away in a thick soup on one end and a slow, steady flame was burning at the other. In between, well, it was anybody's guess what was going on. Katrina was sitting on a stool, a small metallic gadget in her hands. Her eyes were unfocused, but her fingers seemed to be moving on their own, adjusting, spinning, and moving various pieces of metal.

Mr. Hauteman looked fascinated, running his fingers over tubes, following the flow of different colored liquids.

"Did you dream all this, too?" he asked, laughing nervously.

"Yes," Katrina answered, gazing up at a point on the ceiling. Then she continued, her voice flat and dull. "I fell asleep during math class, and I dreamed an angel came to me and told me to hook the wire thingy into the bubbling purple stuff and turn the power on high. It seems to have doubled the power output."

Melinda looked just as out of it as Katrina, hovering above a sickly looking cucumber plant.

That day, the class arrived in the science room to find one radio blaring rap music at the poor cucumber, which was bloated and oozing an unpleasant liquid from what looked like open sores.

"It's Davy, I know it's him," she mumbled, gently stroking the cucumber with one finger as if it were a wounded cat.

"I didn't touch your stupid plants!" shouted Davy, and when he shouted every piece of furniture in the room shook. "And even if I did, that's no reason to mess around with my project!"

Davy's gerbils were gaining weight fast now, faster than they should. They were as round as they were long. And all of them were gaining weight, both the vegetable group and the meat group. Still, none of the food that Davy was leaving for them had been touched.

"Hey, what are these yellow crumbs?" Davy called out, leaning his head right into one of the cages. We all gathered around. Sure enough, there was a scattering of bright yellow crumbs all along the bottoms of both cages. Davy poked at a few of the crumbs with a finger, and suddenly he uncovered the corner of a piece of paper buried under the wood shavings that lined the cage.

"It's a note!" screeched Cherilyn. Davy pulled it out and read it aloud.

"How would you like to be put in a cage and stuffed full of hot dogs? Food isn't science to you, it's an obsession. The Angel of Science."

"Hey, what's an obsession, and do I get free

hot dogs for doing it?" Davy looked at Mr. Hauteman hopefully.

Mr. Hauteman grabbed the note and read it to himself, then looked up at the class.

"Ever since we started work on the science fair, this class has been the last people in the room in the afternoon and the first people in the room in the morning. Whoever is pulling these stunts must be in this class."

Everyone now looked suspiciously around the room. At that moment, I bet we all looked guilty.

"I don't know who is doing this," Mr. Hauteman continued, "but they had better stop before I catch them. The fifth grade science fair is a great tradition in Sanbornton Elementary School. I myself won it when I was your age, and the scholarship helped me become the man I am today." He pulled himself up to his full height, which still wasn't quite as tall as Davy.

Jimmy started to snicker. Davy's mouth started to twitch and his eyes began to water. Katrina coughed to cover up a little laugh. Melinda glared at Katrina with such fire in her eyes that Cherilyn couldn't hold it in any longer and burst out laughing. That set the rest of us off and we laughed until we no longer cared about science, or cucumbers, or scholarships, or Angels, or anything.

It was good to laugh, at least while we could.

CHAPTER 6

"They can't be gaining weight!" Davy bellowed, staring down at the baseball-sized gerbils sitting on the postal scale. "They still aren't eating anything."

"Now, Davy," Mr. Hauteman began, trying to sound calm and reasonable, "we know they aren't eating the food you are giving them, but they must be eating something. Let's look at their environment and see if they're eating something you didn't intend for them to eat."

"Are they eating their babies?" asked Benny, trying to be helpful. Three girls screamed in horror.

"Maybe they are eating Twinkies," Cherilyn offered. She was staring at the floor underneath the table where Davy and Jimmy sat.

"What kind of moron would feed Twinkies to gerbils?" Davy shot back.

Apparently, Davy thought feeding gerbils prime rib was much more reasonable. Cherilyn reached under the table and held up an empty Twinkie wrapper.

"That's not mine!" Davy protested. "I've never seen it before in my life. Well, I probably have, I do eat Twinkies, but not in school. Well, not in class at least, I leave 'em in my locker, but still . . ."

"Oh clam up," said Cherilyn. Then in an excited whisper, "Look, there's another note!"

Mr. Hauteman reached for the wrapper, but Benny got there first. He plucked the note out from inside the cage, quickly unfolded it, and read, "Stuffing rodents full of food isn't a biology experiment. If you want to see biology at work, take a look at the rabbits! The Angel of Science."

All eyes turned to the rabbit cage, where four rabbits, one wearing lipstick, one wearing blush, one wearing cologne, and the other with conditioning mousse in its fur, were snuggling into each other and rolling over each other in a big shifting ball.

Cherilyn beamed and looked up at the rest of us.

"Do you see? It's working. The makeup isn't harming them, it's making them more attractive. They like each other."

Suddenly there was a loud squeal and one of the rabbits jumped a full foot straight up in the air, banging its back on the top of the cage. It fell back down, and the pile began to turn and roll with even more energy than before.

"Wow!" said Benny, leaning his face right up against the cage. "They reeeeally like each other!"

CHAPTER 7

The next day, the whole fifth grade class was waiting outside the science room as soon as the school doors opened. Mr. Hauteman got there just before us and held up a hand to stop us. He looked carefully at the door handle before he inserted his key and opened the door.

From the doorway we could hear the metallic twang of a steel guitar, and a high, crooning voice with a Texas accent was singing.

". . . Oh, my best friend died, and I'm crying in his water dish . . ."

"Oh no," Melinda gasped. "Not that. Anything but that."

She ran across the room to the table that held her experiment. Sure enough, one radio was playing country music, and not your everyday country, but real cowboy music.

". . . I cried when my wife left me, and I cried even more when she came back . . ."

Melinda sobbed out loud. I kind of felt like crying, too, and I hadn't even seen her plant yet.

It was the alfalfa. Every single stalk seemed to have just lain down and died, like it had given up on life.

". . . I only have my horse to kiss good-night . . ."

"Aarrgh!" Melinda screamed while spinning around wildly, hands clenched, and staring into every face in the room that didn't turn away in fear.

"Don't look at me!" Davy protested. "I don't even like that junk."

"It wasn't anyone," Mr. Hauteman stated, though he looked confused. "I stuck a hair in the door when I locked up last night, and it was still there this morning, right where I left it. Nobody opened that door. Nobody has been in here. Could you have brushed the dial when you left yesterday?"

"No!" Melinda cried. "I taped the dial down so it couldn't be moved by accident. And if nobody was in here last night, then who wrote that?" Melinda pointed. We all turned.

Written on the wall above the blackboard, in large, red, painted letters, were the words, "Give up now, all you unworthy. Katrina is the real genius here. The Angel of Science."

"Katrina?" Melinda screamed, but she sounded more confused than angry.

We all looked over to where Katrina sat, seemingly half asleep, in front of her experiment. The mixture of apples and goop was bubbling away as usual at one end of the table, but at the other end now there was a bank of six lightbulbs, all burning brightly, a large electric fan blowing, a microwave oven heating up some kind of frozen dinner, and a robot marching sentry around the whole thing. Everything was plugged into an electric panel at the end of the tubes and wires.

"Katrina," Mr. Hauteman started hesitantly, "is your experiment powering all those things?"

Katrina looked up like she had just been woken from a dream.

"Huh?"

"Katrina, your experiment? How did you figure out how to do all that?"

"The Angel told me," she answered. "I was dreaming during lunch yesterday and the Angel of Science taught me all about electricity and how to change direct current to alternating current. You need to do that, you know, to make an electrical outlet."

"I knew that," said Mr. Hauteman, and he sounded a little defensive to me. "Katrina, I think all these notes are starting to upset you and you have started dreaming up this Angel guy, but he isn't real. You know that, don't you?"

We all waited for Katrina's answer, but it was Davy's voice we all heard instead.

"Whoa, man, what gives?"

We all scrambled over to Davy's table and watched as the gerbil cages rocked and bumped until they almost turned over. Gerbils the size of softballs were running laps so fast they were edging halfway up the sides of the cages on the turns.

"Cool," hummed Jimmy. "NASCAR rats!"

"Maybe they changed the channel on Melinda's plants," Benny suggested. "I hear NASCAR fans like that kind of music."

"Don't be a moron," Davy snapped. "How could gerbils get out of the cage, change the radio station, and get back in the cage? Besides," he looked down at his gerbils, "I put a lock on the cages. Not to keep them in, but to keep anyone from opening the cages and feeding them."

I looked at the bars of the cages, and at the holes between them big enough to slip a T-bone steak through. But then, of course, half the gerbils already had all the meat they could eat.

"How did they get huge without eating anything, huh?" Benny snapped back.

"They were eating something! Someone gave them Twinkies . . . and HoHos . . . and Snickers . . ." Davy's eyes got wider and wider as he picked up wrapper after empty wrapper from beside the cage, ten in all.

"Wow, man," Benny breathed. "That's a serious sugar buzz."

"Um, Benny?" Marjorie's voice quavered. "What has your experiment been eating? We all rushed over to Benny's table, then we all jumped back a few feet. The roaches were huge, at least twice the size they had been when Benny first brought them in.

"Wow," hissed Benny. "I bet that's a one megaton cockroach, maybe two."

Mr. Hauteman stepped up and reached for one of the little bomb-shaped models strapped to the back of a roach. He dropped it the second his fingers closed and shook his hand in obvious pain.

"Davy," he yelled, "turn out the lights."

Davy did as he was told and the room dropped into half-darkness. Each miniature bomb and each cockroach glowed a faint green.

"Benny, I thought you said those weren't really radioactive!" Mr. Hauteman was madder than I have ever seen him; madder than the time Jimmy hooked all the legs of a dissected frog to nine volt batteries on a switch and made it do an Irish jig on the lunchroom counter.

"They aren't!" Benny protested.

Mr. Hauteman just pointed to the neon insects.

"They weren't!" Benny corrected himself.

"It was the Angel of Science," Marjorie gasped.

"Whoever did this was no angel," Mr. Hauteman stated. "But he seems to be able to pass through walls or materialize out of thin air. He's more of a phantom, and he's getting me a little spooked.

CHAPTER 8

It was two days before the science fair, and most of the fifth grade of Sanbornton Elementary School was sitting at their desk looking depressed. Most of the experiments were in shambles.

We found out what went wrong with Cherilyn's project. She noticed a funny smell around the makeup she was keeping on her desk and applying to the rabbits. Mr. Hauteman said he thought he recognized the scent and did some experiments. Somehow, a highly concentrated solution of catnip had gotten into all the products, and it was driving the rabbits crazy. Cherilyn tried separating them, but they moped around their separate cages and wouldn't eat, and the experiment had to be abandoned.

Davy's experiment wasn't going any better. He couldn't keep track of the gerbils' weights because all the gerbils were freaking out. It took him all day just to catch one, and when he did he couldn't keep the thing on the scale long enough to get a reading.

Benny's cockroaches continued to grow at an alarming rate, but any thoughts of teaching them to deliver bombs had gone out the window. The roaches had become more aggressive as they grew. They started fighting each other, with the winners eating the losers. Then they started throwing things out of the maze at Benny when he tried to take the glowing model bombs away. Finally, the few remaining mega-roaches ate the bombs and began belching green fumes. Mr. Hauteman was talking about calling in the animal control officers to put the roaches down.

I was still puttering around with my volcano, painting the sides and adding little paper trees along the slopes. It was hard to put a lot of energy into it, knowing it was just a matter of time before the Phantom struck.

Mr. Hauteman asked Jimmy, as he did every day, how his experiment was going, but his heart wasn't in it. I guess he had more to lose from this than the rest of us. Our projects were going to be failures, but the failure of the whole science fair was going to be on his slightly balding head.

Jimmy was still upbeat.

"It's just about ready. I'm going to have the best project in the whole science fair. I can taste that money already!"

At the word "taste," Davy let out a groan. Ever since his food experiment went down the drain, he had been off his feed. He didn't even want to hear the word "food." Of course, Davy off his feed meant he was only eating five meals a day. Davy eats when he is depressed, or happy, or frightened, for that matter.

Melinda raised her head off the desk, where it had been sitting all science period, and mumbled at Jimmy, "Maybe you are the Phantom, huh? Keeping your experiment safely at home, eliminating the competition at school."

"Not all the competition," Benny stated, staring at Katrina, who was looking lost, as she always was these days. Above her bench was a banner that read, "My Prize Student. The Angel of Science."

It had appeared a day ago, and nobody had dared take it down. On the table, a growing collection of electrical gadgets was being powered by a few apple peels and about a mile of tubes and wires. Katrina was screwing on another piece of equipment. What it was I couldn't guess, but she wasn't even looking at her hands as she worked!

"Come on, Katrina, spill it. Where did you get the idea for this? How do you know how to do all this stuff?" pleaded Melinda, who had finally admitted defeat and packed the carcasses of her dead plants up and taken them home.

Katrina looked spacey. Her words seemed to come from far away. "I don't know where the idea came from. I fell asleep in study hall today, and I dreamed the Angel of Science told me to add this whatchamacallit here to the purple doohickey, and look, it works." Just then the electric alarm clock rang with an ear-splitting alarm. Everybody jumped, except Katrina, who just went on fiddling with the equipment.

Suddenly a boy in the back of the room gave a gasp, and there was a rustling of paper. Everybody turned and stared silently as the boy slowly walked up to the front of the room and handed Mr. Hauteman a note.

Mr. Hauteman opened the note slowly, swallowed hard, and read in a low, quavering voice.

"Cancel the science fair and give Katrina the prize, or all the rodents are doomed. The Phantom."

Apparently, Mr. Hauteman's new name for the Angel of Science had gotten around, and the Angel himself had adopted it. There had been some talk about Katrina being the Phantom, but she was tired all the time and so out of it that nobody really believed it. But why was this Phantom apparently protecting her experiment and sabotaging the rest?

And how had Katrina suddenly become a scientific genius? She adamantly denied staying up all night studying, but then why was she so tired all the time? She claimed that she was afraid to fall asleep because of all the weird dreams she was having, but all that meant was that she was up all night at home and she fell asleep over and over during school.

Mr. Hauteman now spent all his time grilling kids on their whereabouts like he was some TV detective, but for all his trying he couldn't figure out who the Phantom was. Finally, with the science fair less than forty-eight hours away, he was beaten.

"Well," he muttered, half to himself, half to the class, "at least this won't be a very public disaster. Who would want to come to see one science experiment and a couple dozen catastrophes?"

That's when the thought hit me. Who would want to come see this? Who would want to see so many failures? More importantly, who would need to come see the one success? As soon as

school got out, I ran for home as fast as I could.
I needed to talk to my mom, and to get help from
some of her friends.

Chapter 9

And so came the day of the most memorable
fifth grade science fair in the history of
Sanbornton Elementary School. The school
psychologist had taken all of Cherilyn's rabbits
home to try to solve their rodent anorexia. Davy
had taken all of his gerbils home to try and find
a rehab center that would take sugar-addicted
rodents hooked on junk food. There was a dark
cloud over the whole gym. All around, fifth
graders stood beside the smoking wrecks of their

projects. Most of the parents had stayed away, and it seemed like the only adults in the room were teachers and a couple of burly guys in wind breakers hanging around Katrina's project.

"Bodyguards, I bet," Marjorie whispered to Melinda.

"You mean experiment guards," Melinda whispered back. "I wish I had thought of that."

Katrina took advantage of the failures to grab a few extra tables. She needed the room. She had moved all the beakers, tubing, coils of copper wire, Bunsen burners, and everything else into the gym that morning. She had also upped the ante by setting the peels of two apples boiling at once. The results were impressive. Her experiment was powering an entire home theatre, complete with DVD and wide-screen television, eight stereo speakers, a microwave pumping out piles of nachos, a refrigerator full of soda, and a popcorn maker to boot. Davy was so depressed that he plopped down in the big comfy chair and ate the nachos as fast as they would come.

The place felt like a funeral parlor. Everyone looked like someone had died, but I felt that the bad stuff was yet to happen. It was so quiet that everyone in the room jumped when the doors to the gym opened. In marched the Blue Ribbon Panel of Judges, which meant one of the selectmen, the superintendent of schools, and Mrs. Lissard, the principal.

Mr. Hauteman led the panel around the room. They stopped at every table and sometimes asked a question or two before shaking their heads and moving on. They passed a robot that was supposed to be preparing French fries, but just kept cutting the potatoes until they were a gooey pulp. They passed a model of the solar system where all the planets were bouncing off each other and nose-diving into the sun. They passed a student who actually *had* taught a computer to play chess, but the computer kept saying "Go fish!" and "You sank my battleship!" They were three quarters of the way around when they stopped in front of Katrina's tables. Katrina should have explained what she had done, but she didn't have to. There were murmurs and smiles all around.

"My prize pupil," Mr. Hauteman said with a weary smile.

Just then, a number of things happened at once.

Melinda, who was at the next table over, burst into tears and ran for the girls' bathroom.

A man in gray overalls who was standing nearby leaning on a mop cried, "Why you—" and went after Mr. Hauteman.

Katrina pointed at the man in gray overalls and cried, "The Angel of Science!" and fainted.

The two bulky men wearing dark windbreakers yelled, "Hold it right there!" and grabbed the man Katrina was pointing at.

And Mr. Hauteman stared into the eyes of the man being held and said, "Leonard?"

CHAPTER 10

"You sniveling little worm!" The man in overalls spat at Mr. Hauteman. "Don't you dare take credit for teaching that girl. You couldn't teach a fish to swim!"

The man struggled against the strong grip of the two men who had grabbed him. He looked determined to get his hands on Mr. Hauteman's neck. Mr. Hauteman didn't seem to notice the man's rage; he just stared into the man's face, amazed.

"Leonard?" he asked again. "Leonard Glick? What are you doing here?"

"I work here. If you bothered to pay attention to the poor stiffs who work for a living, you'd already know that," he growled.

It struck me that Mr. Hauteman wasn't the only one who hadn't been paying attention. The man looked vaguely familiar, but I wouldn't have noticed him in a crowd, and I hadn't known his name.

"How long have you worked here?" Mr. Hauteman asked.

"Since we graduated from high school. You went off to college with your science scholarship and I started working here the day after graduation. I've been here ever since. It should have been me with that scholarship! I was the best science student at Sanbornton Elementary

School! If I had won that fifth grade science fair, my whole life would have been different."

Mr. Hauteman's eyes widened.

"You?" he whispered. "You're the Phantom of the Science Fair?"

The man in the overalls, the man named Leonard Glick, threw back his head and laughed.

"Yes, I'm the Phantom. And you are the great science teacher who put on the biggest disaster of a science fair in Sanbornton Elementary School history! Not only that, but your prize student managed to kill all the subjects in her experiment while mine created an energy source that will change the world. Who's the great scientist now? I guess we know who really should have won that science fair when we were in the fifth grade!" And with that, Leonard Glick went into a laughing fit.

"Yours? Your prize student?" Mr. Hauteman looked baffled.

Just then, Mrs. Lissard, our school principal, pushed her way through the gathering crowd of students and parents.

"What's the meaning of this?" she hissed, her pinched face contracting almost to a snout. "Who are these men? And why are they holding our custodian?"

"We're police officers, ma'am," said one of the men, flipping a badge from his wallet. "Escapade here thought this guy would show up, so we came in undercover."

My mom is a dispatcher for the county police. I don't think any police officers would have listened to an eleven-year-old with a wild story about phantoms, but I convinced mom, and she called in her guys. They'd do anything for her.

Mrs. Lissard turned to me. "You knew who the phantom was?"

"No," I answered simply. "But I knew he was Katrina's biggest fan, and since she was sure to win, he was sure to be here."

"What's the charge?" shouted Leonard Glick, struggling in the grip of the two police officers, each of whom must have weighed twice what he did.

"Cruelty to animals," the other officer sneered. "What you did to those gerbils, rabbits, and cockroaches was despicable."

"And don't forget what he did to the plants!" shouted a nearly hysterical voice from the back. I'm sure it was Melinda.

Mr. Hauteman shook his head. "All that to avenge the loss of a science fair decades ago. Was it worth it?"

"Wait a minute," cried Mrs. Lissard. "This was all about some silly science fair more than twenty years ago?"

"Not some silly science fair," cried Leonard Glick. "It was *my* science fair. I deserved to win, to get that scholarship, to go to college, to become one of the greats! I deserved a Nobel Prize for my project, but I couldn't even get first place in an elementary school science fair. Instead, they gave it to this half-sized half wit and his model of the solar system."

Man, I thought, a model of the solar system. I wish I had thought of that. It would have been much better than a volcano.

Benny jumped into the commotion and asked, "What was Mr. Glick's project?"

Leonard Glick stared hard at Mr. Hauteman, daring him to remember.

Mr. Hauteman's face screwed up hard, concentrating. Then suddenly you could see the memory hit him.

"Hypnotism," he whispered.

"No, you dolt," spat Leonard Glick. "You never got it; nobody got it. The project was *teaching* through hypnotism. It was implanting knowledge into the subconscious. It would have revolutionized education. I would have been the greatest scientist of my age. Only those small-minded reptiles who ran the school back then wouldn't let me experiment on a few of my dim-witted classmates. I would have shown them if they had given me a chance. But now, the world will see my vision. I have proved you can teach the most muddle-headed eleven-year-old complex science through hypnosis. I have triumphed!"

And as Leonard Glick fell into another fit of evil laughter, the whole room turned to look at Katrina, who had recovered from her faint and was fiddling absentmindedly with some of her equipment. She looked like she was sleepwalking.

CHAPTER 11

"How?" demanded Mr. Hauteman. "How did you do it? How did you hypnotize this poor girl? How did you sabotage all those other experiments?"

"That was easy," Leonard Glick laughed. "I've worked in this school longer than anyone. I know every air duct, every loose wall panel, every maintenance shaft in the place. I can get to any room in the school without ever setting foot in a hallway, and I can whisper to a sleepy student anywhere without ever being seen. You think this school is your world, but it isn't. It's mine!" He dissolved into maniacal laughter.

Suddenly the doors of the cafeteria burst open and Jimmy appeared, leading three huge bulldogs. All right, the bulldogs were leading him, and he was trying to keep them from pulling him in three different directions on their rope leashes.

"Sorry I'm late," he said. "Fiend had to stop and eat a mailman."

Everyone stopped. Fiend, Mauler, and Brutus had a way of getting people's attention.

"Do those . . . creatures have something to do with your science fair project?" Mr. Hauteman asked tentatively, pointing at the dogs without reaching out too close to them.

"Heck, they *are* my experiment," Jimmy beamed.

He shifted all three leashes into one hand, a precarious hold at best, and pulled a piece of yellow lined paper out of a pocket with the other hand. The paper was covered in his distinctive, huge scrawl. He began to read.

"In 1904, a Russian scientist named Ivan Pavlov discovered that he could train dogs to drool at just the sound of a bell by ringing it just before he fed them. I wanted to see if I could train my dogs to salivate at a smell instead of a sound, even if it is a really bad smell. So for the past six weeks I have been putting their food under something that really stank so they would get the connection. Bad smell equals food."

Mr. Hauteman somehow looked surprised, disgusted, and interested all at the same time, the way only an elementary school science teacher can.

"Did you train them to salivate over any bad smell?"

"No, just one particular smell."

"Which one?"

"Benny sweat. I've been stealing Benny's sweaty socks for months." Jimmy pulled a sock out of another pocket and held it up for all to see.

But we weren't looking at the sock. We all looked at Benny, whose eyes now were fixed on those huge, snarling dogs. He looked nervous. He looked scared. He started to sweat. Everyone dove away from him.

As soon as the beads of sweat appeared on Benny's forehead, and dark spots formed beneath his armpits, the dogs leapt.

"Yeoooooowwwwww!" Benny screamed, as he scrambled over a table and rocketed out the door, the slavering dogs hot on his heels.

EPILOGUE

Believe it or not, Jimmy Whitehorse won the Sanbornton Elementary School Fifth Grade Science Fair, and the thousand dollar educational savings bond. He's still trying to find a way to sell it for hard cash, and knowing him, he just might do it.

Of course, there were not many experiments left standing by the time the judges made their choice. Benny had little to show for his work but some murderous cockroaches and a number of holes in his pants from bulldog teeth. Melinda's plants were dead. Davy's gerbils were all in sugar-addict rehab. Cherilyn's rabbits were being treated for depression. Marjorie had only her notes and a big hole. And Katrina's experiment, though impressive, was disqualified because it was entirely an adult's idea, and a mentally unstable adult at that.

And who won second prize? Me. As it turned out, my experiment was so boring that the Phantom saw it as no threat and left it alone. There was no third place, because nobody else completed their experiments.

So they awarded me the second prize, a free dinner for four at Steak Through the Heart, and the third prize, a month's worth of hot chocolate at Joe's House of Joe, as well. I guess sometimes it pays to be the most boring kid in the most boring town in the most boring state in the country.

So what will I write about next? Maybe I'll tell you how I killed the Old Man of the Mountain. (It's a big rock, not a person. Jeez, lighten up!) Or maybe I'll tell you about the Great Wrestling Fever of Sanbornton, New Hampshire. Of course there is still that funny little story about the moose eating all the ballots at a town election, but mom still says it isn't safe to tell that while "the heat is on," whatever that means. I guess when you live in a town this dull, people remember every little mistake for a long time. After all, nothing much ever happens here.

Bye for now.

—Escapade Johnson.

ABOUT THE AUTHOR

Michael Sullivan is a storyteller, juggler, chess instructor, librarian, and former school teacher who grew up in small-town New Hampshire, and now lives in Portsmouth, New Hampshire. He has worked with kids in many settings, from summer camps to the Boston Museum of Science, and is rumored to have once been a kid himself. He is the author of the book *Connecting Boys with Books*, and speaks across the country on the topic of boys and reading. In 1998, he was chosen New Hampshire Librarian of the Year.

Visit Michael's website at:

http://www.talestoldtall.com

OTHER CHILDREN'S TITLES
BY MICHAEL SULLIVAN

Escapade Johnson and

Mayhem at Mount Moosilaukee

Escapade Johnson and

The Coffee Shop of the Living Dead

Escapade Johnson and

The Witches of Belknap County

The Sapphire Knight (The Bard series)

DATE DUE